DEDICATION

This book is for the women of the world. Every day I am
shown the definition of strength, beauty and majesty through
my interactions with phenomenal women.

The first one being my mother.

Lyrically Speaking Again

Ms. Paradox

CONTENTS

ACKNOWLEDGMENTS

This year more than ever I have to thank my support network. My mother and aunts have created a pyramid of strength, love and support around me that is almost impenetrable unless you have the best intentions towards me.

I would also like to acknowledge my daughter. A bright, inquisitive, forthright child who holds me to account and causes me to look at the world differently.

And finally, someone very special who inspired and encouraged me many times over. I call him Baby Boy DTS.

Motivation

As a life coach, it is my job to motivate people. To get them to perceive their true potential, believe in themselves and then achieve their dreams.

PERCEIVE – BELIEVE - ACHIEVE

YES, YOU CAN

I know it is hard to think that you can
To always feel that your dreams will come true
To have absolute belief
That your power shines through

You are amazing
You're one of a kind
Yet sometimes we all
Act like we're blind

We let the power of doubt creep in
We forget to go looking
for the strength that's within

So believe when I say
Because I know the truth
You're going to succeed
You will get through

ACHIEVE

Nerves are nothing
Except distractions
Stressful situations
Provoke a reaction

Take some time
To quell your fears
Close your mouth
Use your ears

Assess the place
You find yourself
Trust only you
And no one else

You have the skills
You have the strength
To stand the trial
To go the length

Today you'll find
You will succeed
Because today you'll
Achieve the best you can be

YOU CAN

It's a brand new day to be amazing
A brand new day to share your light
A time to say you do believe
A time to say you can achieve

Because belief it lays the root
To plant a thriving tree
A tree of dreaming and of wealth
A tree of joy, good cheer and health

So feed your tree with positive thoughts
No time for ifs and buts
So be you woman, be you man
It's time to say I CAN

YOU CAN - 2

I do believe it is that time
The time for us to rise
To take our rightful places
A time to claim our prize

The prize of positivity
The prize that spurs us on
Because when we say our mantra
We will know that we have won

What is this secret recipe?
This mantra that you quote
It's time to say that Yes You Can
To fill your heart with hope

You can
You will

LEGEND

You're stronger than you think
You're bolder than you know
You can do whatever you want
And take yourself where you want to go

Sometimes dreams
Are tough to get
Tough to achieve
Until they're met

You're a legend
You're one of a kind
But disappointment
Has made you blind

Open your eyes
You're ready to go
To achieve your dreams
Be more than you know

YOU ARE GREAT

I believe that you are great
It's a belief borne of love, not hate
I'll push you hard to get your dreams
I'll be quite harsh, or so it seems

I'm your biggest fan
I'm here through thick and thin
I'll cheer you on and hold your hand
So you won't give in

Sometimes it will seem hard
Impossible in fact
So it's time to stop thinking
It's time for you to act

Listen to my chanting
You'll hear it in your ears
The voice that tells you to go on
To overcome your fears

TALL

Stand tall and strong
It won't be long
Until you reach the top

It's time to fight
And claim your rights
Keep going please don't stop

Set standards high
Straight to the sky
And never let them drop

So remember I say
My message is bright as day
"Keep striving to the top."

Letters from the Heart

Sometimes when I am overcome by emotion and feel unable to express myself directly, I pen secret letters to those who are close. I may not be able to say the words, but my letters help me manage my emotions.

LETTER TO MY DAUGHTER

Dear Daughter

I've watched you grow with a sense of pride that rivals every other emotion that I have ever experienced. As we take this journey together and I learn about motherhood and parenthood I am always humbled to watch you reflect my best and worst traits.

You are a fierce girl blossoming into a strong willed and strong minded young lady. I see you advocate for the things that you believe in, and my heart swells with pride.

Your most recent discussion with me was about the potential banning of hijabs in public places in the UK. Your idea was that we should all wear scarves as well to show our solidarity with the women affected and to stand as one against the potentially unfair decision.

Where did you get your activism? I don't know, maybe it is osmosis, maybe you are inherently a defender of liberties.

I watch you grow, and I watch your interests change, and your personality takes shape, and I wonder what you will become. I wonder which profession will beckon you. I have hopes and dreams for you but these are not yours, and I am mindful not to foist requirements on you that may diminish your natural flair and talent.

My dream for you will always be to have a life that you enjoy. To find your calling and your passion and to have the strength and courage to follow that calling even if it seems to be against the grain of everyone else's expectations.

My promise to you is that I will support you and give you the life that enables you to explore many different avenues so that when the time comes for you to answer that call you can do so with minimal regrets and maximum confidence.

I love you, my sweet, sweet girl.

Your Mama xxx

ANOTHER LETTER TO MY DADDY

"To feel loss is a human trait, I wish I wasn't human."

Dear Daddy

It's five years since you have been gone and I feel the pain as if it was yesterday. Well, when I say I feel the pain I only allow myself to feel it sometimes. Most of the time I pretend that you're in Guyana, and I'm in England. You see I'm not very good at dealing with pain and emotions, so I just pretend and play make believe.

I'm working on that, the ability to accept that you're gone. A big part of that process was going home to Guyana knowing that you weren't going to be there to collect me from the airport. Knowing that you weren't going to be around to listen to my stories and give me your opinions.

So there I stood at Timerhi sniffing the night air and half expecting you to come and get me, but you weren't there.

Maybe that's why I had a headache that first night. A crushing pain in my head that wouldn't shift. I kept busy during that first trip back without you. Until the Wednesday morning when I went to visit your grave.

Until the moment I got there, I was saying that I was going to visit you. I couldn't quite remember how to get there, but fate intervened and when we stopped to ask for directions we were actually next to your final resting place.

Finding your spot was easy, and as I stood there, I felt nothing. I didn't feel at home. I wasn't visiting you because you are gone.

When I want to feel close to you, I have to focus on the feeling from within. I have to look for and notice signs that you're around because you aren't in that cold hard tomb.

Afterwards, I felt strangely free. Free of the fear of the unknown. I had conquered my fear. Later that night I wept for you again. One of a handful of times that I have allowed myself the indulgence of weeping.

So Daddy there you go. An account of my journey back home, my journey back to you.

Until we "speak" again.

I love you endlessly.

R

LETTER TO MY BOO

Words don't seem adequate to tell you how I feel about you.
With each passing day, I get more and more attached to you, and
I feel thankful that we decided to take this step.

Moving from friendship to relationship is a big step. On the face
of it, it seems to be fairly simple. With a shared past and lots of
shared memories it seemed easy to say that from this day forth
we were together but it wasn't.

We both had so much to think about before we took this step but
I'm glad that each thought turned into a step closer to the bliss
that we share.

Life hasn't been easy for either of us. Our paths moved from
being close to each other to going in completely different
directions. In a way, I feel like we were co -existing in a parallel
universe.

So close
But yet so far
But now together
Forever!

R xxx

LETTER TO ME AND POSSIBLY YOU

Dear Me

I wanted to talk to you about standards. Why is it that you set yourself almost impossible standards? You can't please everyone, and you can't do everything.

I challenge you only to do the things that meet one of these three criteria:
- It makes you happy. Anything that feeds your soul is a definite keeper
- It keeps you and your child. If you make a good honest living from it, keep doing it
- It feeds your dreams. Life isn't just about where you are now. You have to think about the future. If it moves you closer to achieving your dreams, then keep it.

Anything that doesn't fit into one of those categories needs to be out of your life. Take some time, assess, reprioritise, exhale and move forward.

You know you can do it. You know you will do it. You're an amazing woman.

From Me

LETTER TO THE OTHERS

Dear Others

About a year ago I finally made peace with the fact that I was date raped by my ex-boyfriend. I finally found the courage to utter the words out loud and unequivocally state that I was raped.

For a long time, I thought it was my fault, and I thought that the lines were blurred. I thought somehow that my emphatic no and my clear statements about not wanting to have sex weren't enough because I was in his house.

I blamed myself.

So this letter is for anyone else who has been sexually assaulted. Anyone else who is hiding in the shadows because they aren't sure that there is support for them. Anyone else who is suffering because they feel like their experience is a grey area.

I am here to tell you that there is no grey area. Even if you have told yourself that you're ok the way that I did, there's a very real chance that you aren't ok. Locking the experience into a vault of bad memories won't work forever. You are causing more damage to yourself.

Think about if you were supporting someone else who went through this experience. Would you tell them to stay quiet? Would you tell them to blame themselves? Take responsibility for the lack of control exhibited by the person who hurt them?

NO! you wouldn't. Your desire to protect and nurture would make you stand up for what's right for that person you love.

Well, it's time to love yourself. Tell someone. Share the burden. Say the words. You deserve to move forward not mark time. I know it's hard. It took me almost twenty years to tell my loved ones. A long time to recognise the devastating effect that it had on me.

But I did take the step. I did tell, and now I'm moving forward.

The sun is on my face, and the darkness doesn't visit so much anymore.

So to all you others, I send my love and support.

Razor Sharp

Some people say my tongue is razor sharp. I get straight to the point, and I say what I think. I don't hold back and like my friend Sonia always says to me "That MOUTH!"

DEAR JOHN

Dear John
I wrote in the letter
I found someone else
And he treats me better

I found a new lover
To satisfy my need
He gives me it good
Quenches my greed

I used to think
That you were the best
Until I found my new boo
And gave him the test

Took him on
My freaky tour
Teased him and touched him
Till he begged me for more

He is all
That a man should be
Begging for pussy
Down on his knees

When he teases
He makes me shiver
And when he hits it
He makes me quiver

So even though
Your name isn't John
I hope after this letter
That you are gone

I'M DONE

Pack your shit
Cos we are through
After all these years
I've had enough of you

Poking and prodding me
At your leisure
Being your mistress
Giving you pleasure

It took me awhile
To decide that we're done
To take away my goodies
And end your fun

Thought I would miss it
After all this time
Thought it was your dick
I needed to climb

But in reality
That wasn't true
So like I said
I'm done with you

ANGER

The anger is inside me
The anger never stops
It ebbs and flows
I think it goes
Then it rises to the top

The anger is around me
Raging like a fire
I must succumb
Till it is done
Or I'll end up on a pyre

The anger is outside me
I'll make them pay the price
It now is free
So let me be
Don't want to tell you twice

The anger is in charge now
No time for turning back
My heart is hard
It's marked my card
And turned my soul pitch black

BULLSHIT

No more bullshit
Was what I said
As I looked at the sky
Above my head

Time for starting up afresh
Making new beginnings
Time to be a good girl again
And stop with all the sinning

I've had enough of sex and booze
More than I can handle
Had all the men and drinks I want
I'm hotter than a candle

Time to cool
Like frozen ice
Stop being a bitch
Start being nice

Love

Somewhere behind my tough exterior lies a romantic.
A soft-hearted woman who enjoys the first flush of love
and all the hope that it brings

VOWS

I can place my head
In your loving arms
Because right here
I feel no harm

My protector and soul mate
My lover and friend
You were there at the beginning
And you'll be my end

My last
My final
And all that I need
I'm no longer in charge
I will follow your lead

No need to be boss
I give you my hand
Forever more
By your side, I will stand

Your strength and stability
Set you apart
That's why now and forever
I give you my heart

TRUE LOVE

I wasn't expecting it
I thought that love was lost

I'd been hurt and battered
My heart was in tatters

So I came home with work on my mind
Couldn't believe that true love I'd find

In front of my face
Yet hidden from view

I found my true love
Can't believe I found YOU

MORNING GOODBYE

Good morning boo
I say to you
Every single day

I wish you well
Inhale your smell
And wish that you could stay

Lying with me safe and warm
Where I can keep you safe from harm
Keep the wolves at bay

But alas I can't
So ask I shan't
While I send you on your way

STRENGTH IN TWONESS

It's a bright new day
And I want you to know
You're a beautiful man
And together we will grow

Our bond is unbreakable
We make a good team
So let's get this thing started
Move forward with full steam

I'm behind you
All the way
Whatever you need me to do
Please say

And don't forget to have a great day

MY STRENGTH

It isn't always easy
Being who you are
Life can be tough
And leave many scars

But the way that you have risen
Fills my heart with pride
Because I know firsthand
That it wasn't an easy ride

To see the man that you've become
Weakens both my knees
It's you I can depend on
Because you do it all with ease

MY FAVOURITE GUY

Laughter and smiles
Are balm to my soul
When I heard you happy
It made me whole

The smile you give
When I'm around
Could light up a village
A county, a town

When I'm with you
I haven't a care
Although mostly hidden
My dimples appear

Your eyes smile too
When you're in a happy place
It's so heartfelt and
You're filled with so much grace

I never thought I'd find you
My angel here on earth
A man who takes me seriously
Yet fills my heart with mirth

So smile again
My favourite guy
I need a bit
Of what money can't buy

STRENGTH IN LOVE

The strength of our love
Is not just time
It's whatever we conquer
The mountains we climb

Take my hand
I'll hold you tight
I'll never let go
Because it feels so right

I'll never let go
Your mine
I'm yours

And until forever
My love it pours

Musings

The inspiration to write is triggered by all sorts of things. Sometimes the most mundane topic will ignite a fire ......

WORDS

Words flow abundant
Out of my soul
Wordplay is my life
It makes me whole

Unscrambling letters
My opinions seem pointed
Creating lyrics
My thoughts are disjointed

I grab them like butterflies
Darting around
My words start to tumble
Creative lyrics abound

To catch them all
Is the challenge I take
Not writing them down
Will be my mistake

I scramble for pens
Notebooks as well
As the words pour out
And my story I tell

PANDAMA

The wine was delicious
The wine was sublime
The hosting was gracious
We had a good time

The jamoon, the boulanger, even the pepper
Although to be honest the sorrel is better

Pandama's a place where you go to unwind
There's no better place to relax that you'll find
Communing with nature, letting go of the past
Making sweet memories that surely will last

It's a wondrous place surrounded by trees
You let go of inhibitions and find that you're free
The creek will beckon you to take a quick dip
You'll splash, and you'll turn and maybe do flips

I'll never forget that place that we found
And I'll think of it fondly until next time around

MOTHER'S DAY

a **M**atriarch, she rules with love and grace
Opening her heart to kith and kin
Taking the time to see what's within
Hearts and minds of those that she loves
Encouraging, supporting and pushing us forward
Relishing our triumphs as her only reward

GONE

"To feel loss is a human trait.
I wish I wasn't human ...."

You were there
But now you're gone
I can't help wondering
What I did wrong
To end you're not really started life
To cause myself this emotional strife
Was it the heavy stuff in my hands?
The ever increasingly tight waistbands
Was it my fault?
That you didn't stay
Was it because
I didn't pray?
To cry seems somehow over the top
But the thoughts keep on coming
They just won't stop
So Daddy and I will try again
What's happened now
Won't happen again

INJUSTICE

Injustice is a thing
I find it hard to swallow
I think the ones who cause it
Are often very shallow

My heart it beats with anger
When travesties unfold
The rage is not just burning hot
It smolders till I'm cold

I stand up to the bullies
Though sometimes it is hard
I observe and notice what they do
I always mark their card

My role in life I do believe
Is to end these unfair things
It's not for judges or the law
It's with me it must begin

Teasers

A collection of short stories and novel extracts
*****Sexually explicit content and language******

The Pussy Principles

A raunchy collection of my writing dedicated to my pussy. A gift from the universe I have learnt her preferences, likes and dislikes. She is a source of pleasure and confusion.

With her, I am not always in control. The battle for domination rages between her, my heart and my mind. Sometimes she triumphs in battle, but the war is never over.

Alone Time

Many women don't admit that they masturbate. It's a taboo subject which it shouldn't be. The first pussy principle is that you can't please someone else unless you can please yourself. Women who please themselves are more likely to achieve orgasm with a partner and all the men I have spoken to tell me that they enjoy watching their woman pleasure herself.

So let's explore what happens when women have alone time!

As she closed the window and pulled the curtains, she felt the familiar tightness. Her nipples were swelling, and she could feel them puckering under her t-shirt. As the curtain swished past her nipple, she let out an involuntary groan and imagined that it was his hand brushing past her in the kitchen.

The unbidden memory of him didn't help, and she reached under her t-shirt to caress her nipple. Incredibly it grew even harder, and she quickly dropped her hand knowing that she wouldn't enjoy it until she was lying in bed.

A few moments later she padded into her bedroom closing the door behind her. Tonight she would sleep naked to give her hands the freedom to roam her body untethered. As she stepped out of her underwear, she was startled to see a wet patch had been growing, and she gingerly rubbed herself unsurprised when her finger glistened with the light juices that she had begun to excrete.

She shivered slowly growing accustomed to the coolness of the room. Laid on the bed were her tools. A sleek specially made stainless steel vibrator, its clinical appearance disguising the fact that it was her favourite source of pleasure. She also eyed the nipple clamps knowing that tonight she would need the pleasurable pain that they inflicted. Last was her special oil. A blend of lavender, jasmine, rose and almond oils the smells both relaxed and stimulated her and were perfect when she wanted to have a night to herself.

It was time for her to start her preparation. She picked up the oil, flicking it open with her nails and squirting a generous amount into her outstretched palm. Rubbing her hands together briskly she warmed the oil before spreading it liberally across her whole body. First her legs, slowly rubbing her thighs in and out carefully avoiding her pussy. Then her stomach, back and arms before she started rubbing circles around her breasts. She studiously avoided her nipples although she could feel them straining for attention. Then she slowly brought her fingers to pinch them. They puckered more, and she smiled as they communicated their approval of her actions. She rubbed them continuously almost bringing herself to the brink of orgasm but knowing she wanted to wait until she was comfortable to let go of the tension building in her.

Just as she felt the pressure building, she stopped abruptly. She needed to get comfortable. She let herself fall across the body and positioned her body so that her knees were up. She grabbed the bottle of oil again, this time squirting it directly onto her pussy. She smiled in satisfaction as the cool oil dripped down between the lips and she took a moment to savour the feeling before following the path of the oil with her fingers.

The oil made access easy, and her finger glided straight into the middle of the lips and quickly found their target, her clitoris. She rubbed on it moaning as it increased in length and girth under her stimulation. The oil mixed with her juices created a perfect feeling of silky smooth pleasure.

Her breathing quickened, and she felt the urge to be penetrated. Her fingers slowly inched towards her opening and she grabbed her pussy with her left hand spreading the lips so that she could speed up the rubbing against her clitoris.

It was time.

She reached across the bed grabbing the cool vibrator and licked her lips anticipating the pleasure that was to come. Flicking it on easily she felt a flicker of nervousness as she heard its purring but yearning quickly replaced it. First she pressed the tip of the vibrator against her aching clitoris slowly feeling the vibrations deep within her matching the pulsing of her blood filled nub beat by beat. Then slowly she slid it down and repositioned it against her wet gaping opening.

With a deep breath, she started the vibrator on its journey to her g-spot. With each inch, she squirmed and twisted her hips meeting the insistent plunging with ease as she adjusted her stroke to her growing desires. As her strokes quickened, and her breathing became shallow her imagination raced as she imagined him inside her whispering sweet nothings in her ear as he rubbed her from the inside out. the pressure built up, and as she neared her climax, she imagined him biting her ear and letting out a guttural groan as he too reached the pinnacle of pleasure. With that thought, she let go and lay convulsing as the orgasm overtook her body. As her breathing slowed down to a normal pace, she knew she wasn't finished. Her journey was only just beginning.

Riding the wave of satisfaction, she reached down and switched off the buzzing vibrator careful not to remove t as she enjoyed the feeling of fullness it gave her.

She turned to grab the nipple clamps ready for their pleasure pain combination but had to steady her body movement to ensure the vibrator stayed lodged in her pussy. The continued stretch created by the vibrator kept her pussy throbbing, and she gasped as she pinched her slowly receding nipples with the clamps.

Immediately her nipples grew again, and she glanced at them in wonderment as they stood swollen like a pair of black pearl earrings.

She was tired after her session. Orgasm always made her feel euphorically sleepy and as she imagined him caressing her to sleep she nodded off still full of and clamped by her toys.

Compatibility

Not every dick is compatible with your pussy and even when it is, the dick's owner may not be compatible with you. It's important to understand the Pussy Principle of Compatability because if it isn't all-round compatibility, then it's doomed to fail

LYRICS AND LOVE

I wrote him a poem and waited to hear what he thought.
His response blew me away I wasn't prepared.
I thought he might like it, but I was still a bit scared.
Welcome to our song the lyrics we wrote.
We were both poets in the same boat.

It started with an invite
To taste my pussy galore
And then he laughed and said ....

Him   Baby gimme more
I want to explore
Before we are done
I'll be in your back door
I'll hit it so hard
Rock you to the core
If you fuck me good
don't mean you're a whore

Me   Some say I'm a whore but that ain't the truth
This shit is da bomb
Pussy's tight it ain't loose

Him   You're what I want
Aint letting you go
I chase you like a goose
In hunting I'm pro

Me   Goose is to gander
And hen is to cock
Better believe
I got this shit on lock

Him   I'm immune to loose pussy
           I like it tight
           Fuck wit me, pretty girl
           I'll give you a fright

Me   Give me a fright?
           You think you name duppy?
           I'll make you all dopey
           Like my little puppy

Him   Puppy?
           I don't think so
           When I take hold of you
           I'll never hear no
           My skills are so good
           It's like I control weather
           I'll stroke you up n down
           Soft as a feather
           One touch from me
           You'll be wet like a tsunami
           Part your thighs
           And hear the truth
           Deep in your centre
           My cock won't tell no lies

LETTER FROM PUSSY

Dear Dre

I can't wait to see you. I just wanted to send you this letter to whet your appetite for when we are together again.

I want to touch you from head to toe. First I want to kiss you. I'll devour you as soon as I get you in private. I'll be holding my breath until we get to the hotel.

I want you to kiss me down the neck while I run my hands down your back. I want to imagine your tongue making lines all over my body then I want to slowly take off your clothes letting my lips follow every piece of clothing that I take off.

Then I want you to bend me over and lick from behind my knees all the way up my thighs slowly then let your tongue glide slowly over my clitoris.

I promise I'll be wearing something easily accessible so that you can take what belongs to you. I am lying here imagining that you are here with me.

If you were, I would be kneeling in front of you taking you in my champagne filled mouth. Sucking you slowly while the bubbles trickle over your moist swollen head. You wouldn't be allowed to touch me because I want to be in control and stare deeply into your eyes while you bite your lips the way you do when you are turned on.

I know you won't let me be in control for long. You never do when you are in that mood, but I'll savour the power every minute that I can. Then I'll stand in front of you and stroke my pussy then lick my juices off my fingers before I kiss you deeply letting our juices mix on our tongues.

Damn baby, I can't wait for you to come home. It's been way too long, and my pussy needs you.

Anyway gonna sign off now, just thought a sex letter would be different to the usual emails and sexting that we do.

Lots of love

Me and ya pussy xxxxxx

Pleasure

The next principle is pleasure. Never deny pussy what she wants because a horny pussy is an angry pussy! A horny pussy has no sense of time, place or appropriateness. It is about satisfying the base sexual urges.

I love sex I can't lie, but this love has got me into trouble at times. I remember years ago meeting this guy in a club. I was tipsy but not drunk enough to abandon my senses. He moved behind me as a slow reggae song played, and we swayed in time to the music. I could feel his cock getting hard against me, and I loved the powerful feeling that it gave me. The more he pressed against me, the more powerful I felt and when his lips made contact with my neck I knew that I was falling over the edge.

As the song ended, he guided me to the side of the room, and we sat on a sofa. Me sitting on his lap legs across his and his hand between my legs slowly finding the wet spot that he had created on my black lace underwear. Neither of us cared about whether the barman could see us. He would have been the only person in the room with a view of what we were up to, but we didn't care. As his fingers made contact with my swollen pussy lips, it was like a jolt of lightening had hit me. I started to squirm in his lap hoping that the way I moved would help his fingers to make contact with my throbbing clitoris. In almost seconds my movements were rewarded when I felt his fingers move past my underwear and make contact with my pussy. I started to kiss his neck and moan in his ear. I guess I had pushed him over the edge because he abruptly eased me off his lap and stood up. I felt all confused wondering what I had done wrong and what was wrong with him.

As I blinked attempting to regulate my breathing, he grabbed my hand and said let's go for a walk. I held his hand and walked slightly unsteadily next to him. Not because I was drunk but because I could still feel my pussy throbbing and my panties were bunched between my lips, agonizingly causing my clitoris to tremble.

Once we got outside we went for a walk, hand in hand as we walked past a car park we looked at each other meaningfully and without words, we both started walking towards the car park. We entered a stairwell in the car park and started kissing passionately. Before I knew it, he was behind me and inside me. His cock is straining to dig deeper and deeper into me. I pushed back against him, still able to hear the dull vibration of the music from the club and as the songs beat harder we reached our joint climax.

I saw him twice after that. A couple of days later when we repeated the mind blowing sexcapades and then four years later when I saw a guy I didn't recognise looking at me. I wondered why he was looking at me so intently, but something about the piercing green eyes that stared at me felt familiar, and as I walked past him the penny dropped!

ABOUT THE AUTHOR

Ms. Paradox is an unapologetically open soul who has unleashed her talent to weave stories and spit lyrics on her experiences and observations. Her gritty and provocative style is captivating and challenging.

Her softer pieces are juxtaposed with a raw sexuality that sometimes confuses and proves why she is called Ms. Paradox

Turn over for a preview of her novel Screwed Up Sister out later this year.

Screwed Up Sister

*A novel about one woman's journey
from
Screwed Up
to
Sane!*

NO MORE BULLSHIT

I lay staring idly at the spider web on the ceiling; I mentally prepared my shopping list. I needed some of those nice chopped tomatoes, pasta, vinegar, ketchup, yoghurt and some cornflakes, oh yes and... suddenly the urgent moaning in my ear interrupted my thoughts. I had managed to zone completely out of the unsatisfying sexual encounter that I was having with Joseph, my latest lover.

As I returned to earth with a jolt I had a revelation, I wasn't enjoying this one bit. Here I was laid out on my back making appropriate noises while planning my next trip to the supermarket. Enough was enough. I deserved better. I pushed Joseph off me and hurriedly pulled on my clothes. He looked at me in confusion and asked what was wrong. I looked at him as if seeing him for the first time and said "your crap in bed" and walked out, leaving him limp dicked, confused and ever so slightly angry.

As I left his house and walked to my car, I had a spring in my step. I felt like a new woman, seeing the world for the first time in Amazing Technicolor instead of the hues of grey, which seemed to have taken over my psyche. And it was at that moment I decided to change my life. In a way I guess I had found

73

my amazing technicoloured dream coat, it was just a shame about Joseph!

So, this story charts all the guys who screwed me over, stole a piece of my rainbow and left me in the dull greyness.
Take this journey with me to find out how I became a "Screwed up Sister".

Zavia

PROLOGUE

So where do I start? At the beginning I guess. My name is Zavier Fraser; I was born into a big family number seven of nine children. I was an Army brat and my family moved between London and Guyana as well as visiting Antigua and New York when my father was on individual assignments for short spaces of time.

I was born in Georgetown, Guyana to two loving though very different parents. If I were going to explain their contribution to the woman who I would later become, then I would say that their greatest gift to me was independence. They taught me to work hard, make my own money and make my way in life. My dad's contribution was my annoying, argumentative nature and my mum taught me to be kind and considerate and consider a range of views before making a decision. She also taught me to strive continuously for something more, swim against the tide and make my own path.

Of my nine siblings, two stand out as my favourites although I wouldn't necessarily admit that out loud. Firstly, there is Adam, my brother who is just ten months older than me. Being so close in age we bicker all the time "like cat and dog" our mother says, and we argue about anything and everything. However, regardless of the arguments, he and I are incredibly close. If he needs me, I am there.

My other favourite is Lola, my second eldest sister. As one of the eldest, she ended up being like a surrogate mother to me when things got too hectic for our mother. Somehow Lola never forgot to check on me, even when I was up in my room engrossed in a book. Lola is still my number one sister. We talk almost every day and although she doesn't have children of her own "who needs kids when I got seven of you already" she would say. She is pretty much my second mother.

I remember the first time that I had thrush. I explained to her that I was feeling itchy and uncomfortable like little aliens were poking my vagina. She laughed out loud, told me to get some 0 old. We sat next to each other in the Army nursery and found that we both had names beginning with Z. Both Army brats of fathers who happened to work together we found ourselves often moving to the same locations and as such we built a strong friendship. Zee is more than a friend to me; she is another sister. We have been through thick and thin together.

ROBBIE

I met Robbie when I was 15; he was everything a girl could dream of tall, cute and always a wicked twinkle in his eye. Robbie swept me off my feet with his complete disdain of me and his 'treat em mean, keep em keen' attitude. In my innocence, I thought that I was so hot that he wouldn't be able to resist me. I convinced myself that he would be different with me. Oh, how wrong I was!

I remember the day we met; it was at an amusement park where I had gone to hang out with my friends. Propping up the gates was the usual group of "bad" boys and at the centre of this group was a gorgeous caramel coloured boy I had ever laid my eyes on.

He had low cut hair and grey eyes the colour of slate. His tall, lean body was stretched against the gate, and the earring in one ear twinkled in the sunlight. As I looked at him, I drank in every detail of him like he was a tasty chocolate milkshake. He, of course, didn't notice me drooling over him as he was slouched against the gate eyeing up every girl who passed. Taking them in from ass to toe (their faces never seemed relevant to Robbie. As my grandfather would say, "you don't need to look at the mantelpiece to poke the fire").

Once I had my bellyful of his gorgeous features, I nudged my friend Zee and pointed him out to her. Immediately she started to tell me what a bad boy he was and how he used to date her cousin Tricia until she had caught him with another girl at her own birthday party no less. Her exact words were "That boy makes trouble look like a walk in the park, he is bad news!"

So armed with this stark warning I spent the afternoon trying to put those eyes out of my mind. Zee and I made a pact to try out every ride at the fair, and I was game for the challenge. Halfway through the afternoon, I was giddy having just come off the spinning wheel, so Zee went to get me a drink. I stood leaning under the shade of a large palm tree, enjoying the warmth of the indirect sunlight with my eyes closed. Suddenly I felt a hand moving the hair from my face while whispering "I wondered if it was real". I jumped to the side a little and opened my eyes quickly. There stood my caramel Adonis, Robbie, in the flesh staring at me in a way that made my stomach do little flips. I smiled at him and said, "of course it's real, and who gave you permission to check it for yourself?" He chuckled and calmly said, "I do what I want when I want and to whom I want". The mere sound of his voice was enough to make my spine tingle and the added effect of what he had said almost made me faint. He smiled enigmatically and asked me my name, and I swear it took every ounce of my brainpower to remember my name, "Z Zavia"

I stammered, "Zavia? Wow, what kind of name is that?" he said with a confused look on his face, "I mean if you don't wanna give a brotha your name just walk away. No need to make shit up" he said while starting to walk away. "No, that really is my name", I said. "I'm named after my dad Xavier, but obviously, I needed the female version, and the registrar mixed it up so here I am Zavia!"

He turned and looked at me probably to see if I was making it up. I guess I passed the test because quick as a flash the charm was back on full power. "Well Zavia," he said, "I like the look of you. I think I'll be getting to know you better. I....." Before he could finish his sentence, I heard Zee exhale loudly as she barged in front of me with her eyes blazing and her hands on her hips. "Oh please fool, if you think that I'm going to let you have anything to do with my best friend then you are clearly living in an F-A-N-T-A-S-Y." She slowly spelt out the word poking him in the chest with each letter. At first, he looked affronted but then he started to laugh and said "now little girl I've told your friend already that I do what I want when I want and to whom I want. You're not going to change that so just move out of my way and let me finish my conversation".

Zee grabbed my hand and pulled me away before I could say anything more to him, I was disappointed, but she looked so

79

angry that I followed her wordlessly. We didn't see Robbie or his friends for the rest of the day, and I struggled to hide my disappointment. Zee spent every minute telling me stories about how Robbie had pressured girls into having sex, cheated on them, broke their hearts and used and abused them. With all of this negativity ringing in my ears, I decided to go home early after promising Zee that I would have nothing to do with Robbie. I explained that she had interrupted our conversation before we could exchange details so there was no chance that we would be in contact.

The next day I was busy baking cupcakes for a school bake sale when the phone rang. As I was near it, I answered and was surprised when a male voice asked for me. I was breathless but trying to sound cool. "Who is this?" I said. "It's Robbie. What are you up to?" "I'm baking" "hmm when am I gonna get a chance to taste your cake?" "Whenever you want", I said excitedly before figuring out that his words had a double meaning. He laughed and said, "I'm looking forward to it". We talked for almost an hour that day, finding out about each other. We were both Chicago Bulls fans and loved Michael Jordan but had opposing views on music and food. By the end of the conversation, I was smitten and didn't hesitate when he suggested that we keep our conversations secret so that we didn't upset Zee. It never occurred to me that it might be a ploy to ensure that he could talk to as many girls as he wanted without us finding out about each other. A week later and I had met Robbie a few times for a quick chat, and we had shared a stolen kiss. I was even more smitten. Our meetings were still a secret as he insisted it would be less hassle than upsetting my best friend and I agreed with him.

We were fast approaching the end of the Summer Term, and I was looking forward to the annual school fair, which culminated in a party for thirteen to eighteen-year-olds from all over Georgetown. Zee and I had spent weeks deciding on our outfits, and we had changed our "perfect" hairstyles, at least, ten times during the planning phase. I was so excited, expecting this to be my "coming out" event with Robbie, who I knew usually attended the fair. I naturally assumed we would go together as we were now boyfriend and girlfriend.

On the morning of the fair, Zee and I went to the hairdressers, as we sat under the gigantic hair dryers with our rollers I heard a familiar voice to my right. I looked over and saw Robbie talking to one of the other girls getting her hair styled. I pushed my head as far upwards as I could reach so that my face was obscured by the hood of the dryer. I didn't want him to see me with these stupid rollers, which Miss Simone insisted that I use, even though, my hair was naturally curly. I observed him talking to the girl for about ten minutes, laughing and showing those oh so perfect teeth as he smiled widely. Then he kissed her on the cheek before leaving the shop. I think my heart stopped for a split second, and I felt nauseous and upset. I wanted to know what was going on. I wished I was brave enough to confront him but the combined fear of how he would react and how Zee would react when she figured what I had been hiding from her kept me silent. I'd have to wait until I got home to telephone him and get some answers.

It seemed like an eternity waiting for my hair to finish and even longer to wait for Zee who had decided at the last minute that she wanted a cut as well.

By the time I finally walked through my front door I was a bag of nerves. I made a beeline for the phone, dialling Robbie's number while I walked to my room. Luckily he was the one who answered the call "Hey baby wassup?" he said to me as he heard my voice. He sounded completely unflustered like everything was normal and for a split second, I wondered whether I had dreamt about him being in the Salon. "Don't baby me", I said. "I saw you at the hair salon earlier, laughing with that girl and kissing her and you have the nerve to ask me wassup?" I could feel myself getting hysterical, so I stopped talking and waited for his response. Then he started to chuckle "baby girl calm down, that girl is my cousin. I noticed her in the shop, and as I haven't seen her for a long time, I stopped to say hi. You can ask her if you want but be warned that she cannot stand insecure people so she may be really rude to you!" "Your cousin?" I whispered feeling like an idiot. I was so relieved to hear his simple explanation. "Yeah, my cousin. So if that was all you wanted, I'm gonna get off the phone. I got stuff to do before the fair" and click I heard the insulting sound of the ring tone in my ear.

After the call, I packed my bag and went to Zee's house to get ready for the fair. I had hoped to arrive at the fair with Robbie, but I couldn't ask him after our argument. As I walked in I felt dejected but Zee's enthusiasm was contagious and as we dressed it rubbed off on me and I felt a stirring of excitement. Soon we were ready. I wore a short, tan dress with matching cowboy boots and beaded jewellery draped all over me. The dress skimmed my ample butt and cinched in at the waist. My hair was in big loose ringlets and strategically swept off my face with a feathered hair band. Zee wore a short denim jumpsuit with gladiator sandals and bronze jewellery to complete the Roman look. Her new hairstyle showed off her slender neck, and her skin was a glowing dark brown from the hot Guyanese sun.

At the fair, Zee and I were making quite an impression. I could feel eyes on us everywhere we went, and I noticed quite a few of the guys from school looking our way and nudging each other. I had to admit Zee, and I looked good, and all the effort and planning had paid off, but the one person who I wanted to see was nowhere in sight. I convinced Zee to accompany me to the athletic track under the guise of wanting to check some market stalls, but I was hoping to bump into Robbie.

As we crossed the track I felt someone tapping my shoulder; I turned around with a smile expecting to see Robbie's cute face, but instead, there stood JJ one of our school's star basketball players. He was a year ahead of us, and I had to admit that he was very good looking. His parents were rich and prominent in the Indo-Guyanese social circles. They lived in a big house, and I had heard that JJ was the sole heir to a significant amount of land and some mines in the "Interior". Despite all the positive things that JJ had going for him and his broad, dimpled smile, I still felt a stab of disappointment because he wasn't Robbie.

As he smiled at me, he said, "I just wanted to say hi and to ask you for your number. I've noticed you recently and today seemed like a good day to talk to you, especially with you looking so pretty". I smiled politely at him and said: "I can't give you my number because I have a boyfriend, but thanks for the compliment and you take care". Zee was following this exchange with interest, and she watched open mouthed as I gave JJ the brush off. "C'mon Zee, let's go and close your mouth before a fly goes in it!"

She ran to catch up with me, and I heard her breathlessly asking me exactly who this boyfriend was that I had suddenly acquired. The question stopped me in my tracks, and I cringed as I remembered that I had been keeping a secret from my best friend for almost two months. I turned and looked at her, took a deep breath and then blurted out that I had been seeing Robbie. I rushed the sentence and said "I know you think he's a bad boy, but he's changed. He really likes me, and we're happy together".

She looked at me in complete and utter disbelief tinged with a hint of disappointment. I thought that was hard enough to deal with, but the next words out of her mouth cut through me like a knife "Zavia, we've been friends since nursery. We sat together and played together almost all our lives and not only didn't you trust my judgment, but you also went behind my back for a guy! I can't believe you did this to us. I am so angry and disappointed with you right now. I can't stand by and watch you get hurt. You need to make a choice. It's him or me!" I couldn't believe that she was reacting like this. I told her in no uncertain terms how immature she was and explained that I would not be choosing. She looked at me angrily and shouted "Well I'll make the choice

85

for you. Find a new best friend" and flounced away.

I stood there like a fool, in the middle of the athletics track, watching my best friend's back as she walked away from me. I wondered where the hell Robbie was as I was now alone! After about half an hour, they announced that the party was about to start, so I headed for the gymnasium which had been decorated and had music pumping out of it. As I walked in I bumped into some girls from our class, so I joined their group, happy to chat and dance and get into the party vibe while still looking out for Robbie.

Suddenly I heard a ripple of voices coming from the general direction of the door and saw Michelle, one of the prettiest girls in the school, walking into the party holding Robbie's hand. My mouth went dry, and I blinked a few times hoping that it wasn't him but with each blink my vision of him only got clearer. I moved closer to make sure that it was him, hoping that it wasn't, but it was.   As I inched closer to them, I heard Michelle giggling at something that Robbie was whispering in her ear while he gently stroked her fingers which were interlinked with his.

Each step I took towards them made my heart and feet feel heavy, but I was determined to look him in the eye so that there would be no lies or misunderstandings about what I had seen. As I moved towards them, I noticed Zee across the room, looking from Robbie to me with a quizzical look on her face. I mustered a smile in her direction, but she turned away so obviously I was on my own.

As I stepped in front of Robbie and Michelle, I slipped on some spilt drink on the laminate floor and landed face down at Robbie's feet. When I looked up, Michelle and her friends were sniggering, and Robbie was smiling down at me making no attempt to help me up. Suddenly, I felt an arm pulling me up and found myself looking at Zee as she tried to pull me to my feet. I looked imploringly at Robbie hoping that he would acknowledge me or try to explain his actions to me, but he avoided eye contact and continued to talk to Michelle and her friends.

Zee ushered me towards the bar and looked at me with a shake of her head. "Zee, I'm so sorry that I lied to you. You don't have to say I told you so. I can see what an asshole he is. I'm sorry that I didn't take your word for it when you warned me. I promise I'll never ignore you again." She looked and me and burst out laughing. "I know your crazy ass is gonna ignore me again, but I can't even stay angry at you considering I just picked you up off the floor. I think that was punishment enough don't you?" I looked at her and started laughed too even though my ego was still bruised.

That night I hoped Robbie would call me, but he didn't. The next morning, I waited for my parents to go to church and then dialled his number. When he heard my voice, he didn't even say hi. He asked me why I had embarrassed myself like that in front of his friends. I was livid, "embarrassed myself? That isn't really the issue. What the hell were you doing with Michelle? I thought you were my boyfriend?" "Boyfriend? Are you crazy? I don't go out with girls who don't put out. You were just a potential pussy to me, and clearly you aren't giving that pussy up anytime soon, so I ain't wasting a minute more on your babyish ass." CLICK. That bastard had the nerve to put the phone down on me again. I redialed, but he wouldn't answer, and I was stuck brooding over him for the rest of the day. Over the next week, I tried to call him back a few times but he never answered or disconnected my calls, and finally, I stopped calling for my own sanity.

ABOUT THE PUBLISHER

ROI JELLY Publishing was established in December 2014 to work with writers who have a story to tell but want to retain control of their work.

We work with our writers to provide a bespoke publishing service that meets their needs and budgets.

We are anxious to hear from writers from across the world to discuss how we can help make their work go global. We are also passionate about bringing social issues to light and support various causes.

Email us at roijelly@outlook.com